MW01042046

The
Princess
and the
Giant

By Jordan and Leah Easley
Illustrated by Lisa Christie Leach

The Princess and the Giant
Copyright © 2014 by Jordan and Leah Easley
Published by 5 Fold Media, LLC
www.5foldmedia.com

All rights reserved. No part of this book may be reproduced, stored in a retrieval system, or transmitted in any form or by any means-electronic, mechanical, photocopy, recording, or otherwise-without prior written permission of the copyright owner, except by a reviewer who wishes to quote brief passages in connection with a review for inclusion in a magazine, website, newspaper, podcast, or broadcast. The views and opinions expressed from the writer are not necessarily those of 5 Fold Media, LLC.

Illustrated by Lisa Christie Leach

ISBN: 978-1-936578-74-0

Library of Congress Control Number: 2013946006

I bind unto myself today
The virtues of the star-lit heaven,
The glorious sun's life-giving ray,
The whiteness of the moon at even,
The flashing of the lightning free,
The whirling wind's tempestuous shocks,
The stable earth, the deep salt sea
Around the old eternal rocks.

To Judah.

IN a time and a country long ago and long forgotten, there lived a wise king and a radiant queen, much beloved by their people. The whole kingdom erupted in colorful light when the queen gave birth to a princess, for there was a great show of fireworks that filled the whole dome of the sky. The fireworks danced across the heavens in all forms, from dragons to dogs to daffodils. They lingered long enough for their radiance to sparkle in the eyes of all who beheld them, and then they exploded in roars or barks or whispers. Under the glow and noise of the fireworks, the king and queen spread a wondrous feast for the whole city, full of the best foods. There were soups, puddings, breads, cheeses, fruits, sausages, sweetmeats, pies, and cakes! All these lovely dishes made the guests quite thirsty, and the king and queen's merry fauns scurried to and fro refilling the guests' cups with honey mead and water.

And the dancing! The whole city, young and old, danced the May Dance (complete with rainbow-colored ribbons), the Marooned Sailor Jig (even though no one was marooned on this happy occasion), and the Flight from Orion, which was led by the glimmering, glittering Pleiades. Once in a while someone would miss a step, and everyone would laugh with the fun.

The princess, of course, was unaware of all this celebration. But she knew that her bed was warm and soft and that her father and mother loved her, so her first night in the world was a happy one. The princess smiled and giggled and laughed all night.

The king and queen saw that when the princess smiled, the bedroom lit up with moonlight, and when she giggled, with sunlight. But when she laughed—oh, that was the best of all! When she laughed it was as if the sun and the moon hugged and danced together. So the king and queen nicknamed her "Light Princess."

But under the cover of darkness and the distraction of the party, a beautiful but evil witch slipped into the castle. The pretty witch had long desired to rule the realm herself, but she knew she had no claim to the throne. She had been watching and waiting for a chance to kidnap a royal heir and vanquish the kingdom. Pretending to be a queen from a faraway land with a gift for the newborn, she tricked a kind, but foolish, guard and entered the princess's room. Before the king and queen could stop her, the witch spun a spell of blackness over the child: "You have been marked for the realm of darkness, princess. In the fullness of time, I will return for you and you will become my apprentice. I will teach you the ways of power, and you and I will rule together. We will be beautiful and terrible. Watch and wait." Then the wicked witch departed in a cloud of darkness.

The king and queen were not foolish; they knew that the Light Princess and the kingdom were now in mortal peril. The only chance for the princess and the kingdom to escape the witch's curse was to hide her as far away as possible. They summoned their oldest and dearest friends, Fizzle and Mizzle, the dwarves. When not visiting the palace, Fizzle and Mizzle lived deep in the woods, in a cottage built into the side of a cave. (Dwarves love rocks and caves, finding them safe and cozy.) With broken hearts, the king and queen asked the dwarves to raise the princess in their secluded home. They knew they must never see each other again as long as the princess and the kingdom were in danger, and on the day of the parting, they all wept as they had never wept before.

So it came to pass that the king and queen and Fizzle and Mizzle hid the princess from the schemes of the wicked witch. But a shadow descended over the palace, and, indeed, the whole kingdom. After the Light Princess's departure, the king and his knights rode only black horses and wore only black armor. The royal herald's notes, formerly so cheerful, were now sounded only in minor keys. The queen changed all the palace banners and draperies to black, and she and her maidens wore only black dresses. The subjects of the kingdom, out of reverence and love and mourning, also adopted black garb.

As there were no more fireworks displays, the night sky was never lit by color again. Sometimes the Pleiades twinkled dimly against the blackness, but they never led dances anymore. The fauns brought plain food and drink to the royal table. And so the realm, so colorful on the day of the Light Princess's birth, was shrouded in darkness and shadow.

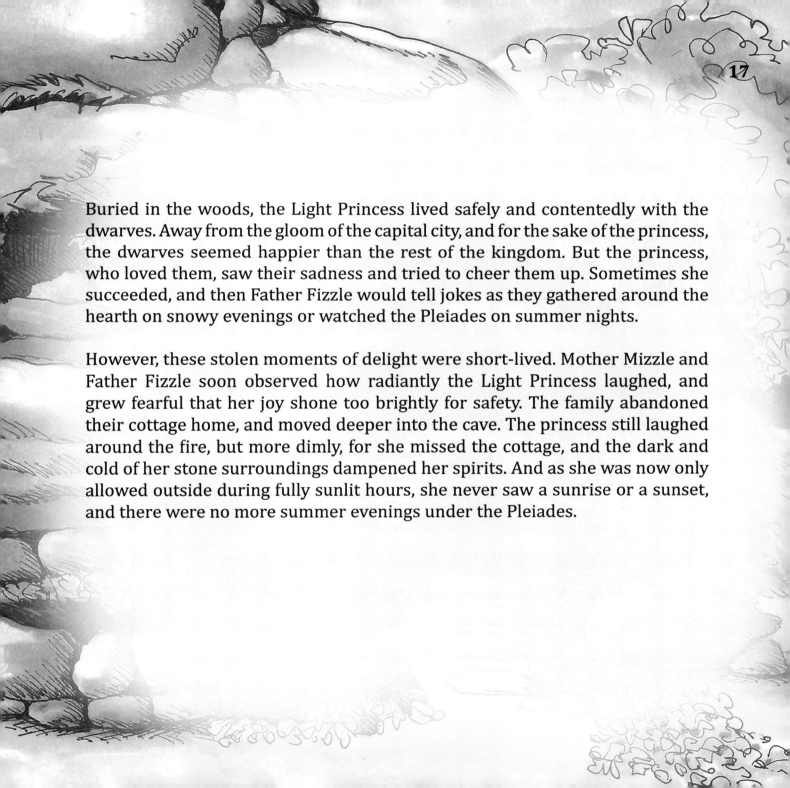

Buried in the woods, the Light Princess lived safely and contentedly with the dwarves. Away from the gloom of the capital city, and for the sake of the princess, the dwarves seemed happier than the rest of the kingdom. But the princess, who loved them, saw their sadness and tried to cheer them up. Sometimes she succeeded, and then Father Fizzle would tell jokes as they gathered around the hearth on snowy evenings or watched the Pleiades on summer nights.

However, these stolen moments of delight were short-lived. Mother Mizzle and Father Fizzle soon observed how radiantly the Light Princess laughed, and grew fearful that her joy shone too brightly for safety. The family abandoned their cottage home, and moved deeper into the cave. The princess still laughed around the fire, but more dimly, for she missed the cottage, and the dark and cold of her stone surroundings dampened her spirits. And as she was now only allowed outside during fully sunlit hours, she never saw a sunrise or a sunset, and there were no more summer evenings under the Pleiades.

Still, the Light Princess grew and grew, and soon she was so tall that she nearly bumped her head on the ceiling as she hummed over the stove or swept the corners of the cave. Each day, as soon as the sun was high, she went to a cool pool under a waterfall to draw water for the garden.

Unbeknownst to the dwarves, when she looked into the pool, she made silly faces and smiled and laughed, and the light that danced forth from her laughter bounced from the water and lit the leaves of the forest with silver and gold. In this way, twelve years passed.

One day, while the Light Princess and her dwarf parents were out picking wild berries near their home, they heard many great thuds crunching through the underbrush of the forest. When they looked up, they gasped. They could not believe their eyes! An enormous billy goat, nearly as tall as a full-grown tree, came bounding right past them through the bushes and the brambles.

But before the Light Princess could catch her breath, something even more amazing crashed into view and stood before them (and nearly stood on them too): a boulder-sized shoe landed square on the roof of their old cottage and shattered the little house with a crunch and a crack. Attached to the foot was a leg, longer than the tallest oak tree, and above the leg was a waist, wider than the widest willow tree, and way beyond the waist—almost into the clouds it seemed—was a great red beard on a great red face.

With a voice like stuttering thunder, the giant bellowed down, "M...m...my sincerest ap...p...pologies, for c...c...crushing your c...c...cottage. I was ch...ch...chasing my r...r...rascally b...b...billy goat B...b...billy, when I s...s...stumbled r...r...right on top of your house! How c...c...can I p...p...possibly p...p...put things r...r...right?"

The Light Princess could not help herself; even though her beloved old home was smashed to matchsticks, she laughed! Her laughter, cool and warm at once, soon had Father Fizzle and Mother Mizzle chuckling too. Even the gentle giant, baffled as he was, began to guffaw to shake the sky. They all laughed until their bellies ached. Father Fizzle and Mother Mizzle cried with relief, for they had not had a good laughing fit for a long time.

Suddenly Mother Mizzle, always the most practical of the three, had an idea. "There is a way you can set things right, Mr. Giant, but it is rather a long story. Our daughter has not even heard it yet, but I believe the time has come. Let us make ourselves comfortable."

So the giant sat down rather clumsily and with a big thud, and the Light Princess and Father Fizzle and Mother Mizzle sat in his very giant lap. While the princess ate the wild berries, Mother Mizzle and Father Fizzle told her all about her birth, the happy party, and the unhappy curse. "Your parents gave you to us for your rescue, but it is time to defeat the witch and break her spell," said Father Fizzle. Then he craned his head toward the giant, and said into the giant's great, red beard, "Mr. Giant, you are so tall that you can see all the kingdoms. Will you bring us to the castle of the wicked witch?"

The giant, though good-hearted, was not very brave, and he gulped. However, as is often the case with giants of his sort, his goodness won out over his fear and he promised to take them, albeit with a very pale face. The Light Princess, although good and brave herself, was also very frightened. She knew she must defeat the witch and save her kingdom, but she felt fear rising from the pit of her stomach. Very timidly, she asked her Mother Mizzle and Father Fizzle, "I don't want to put you in danger, but will you go with me?"

"Of course we will, dear," said Mother Mizzle. "We would never ask you to go alone."

So they began their journey. The giant scooped them up, and all four of them began heading toward a peculiar, faraway spot that seemed to be encased in dark smoke. The journey should have been pleasant, and under different circumstances most certainly would have been. The Light Princess saw more of her kingdom than she had ever seen before. She saw the towering mountains, capped with snow but reaching down into fields of wildflowers, and the low valleys, decorated with foamy pools like the one near her home.

There were wild and mysterious forests and clear sapphire lakes, and very far off, she could just glimpse the sea. The princess saw all sorts of animals—badgers and beavers and bears, robins and rabbits and raccoons, horses and halcyons and hedgehogs—who played merrily, creating a ruckus. The wind blew softly, making the forests dance and bringing the lovely scents of the flora to the travelers. But neither the beauty of the land nor the delight of the animals could help them forget their errand.

Too soon they arrived at the witch's castle. The land was shrouded in a black mist that seemed to suck all the sunshine out of the air. The moment the giant took one great step into the mist, they felt prickling ice run along their necks, and they smelled withering cabbage. They strained their ears, but only cold silence boomed back.

Suddenly a shrieking voice, like a thousand angry rats, sliced through the mist and echoed all around them: "I have been waiting for you, Princess. All those marked for darkness must return home. Your black throne awaits you. Come further into to my midnight realm." The giant gulped. The dwarves shuddered. The princess clenched her jaw. They walked slowly forward.

"I have no use for your companions," cried the voice again. "Leave them behind lest I grow angry." They halted, and strained through the mist to read each other's faces. Though they were shaking, they all nodded at once and the giant took another step forward.

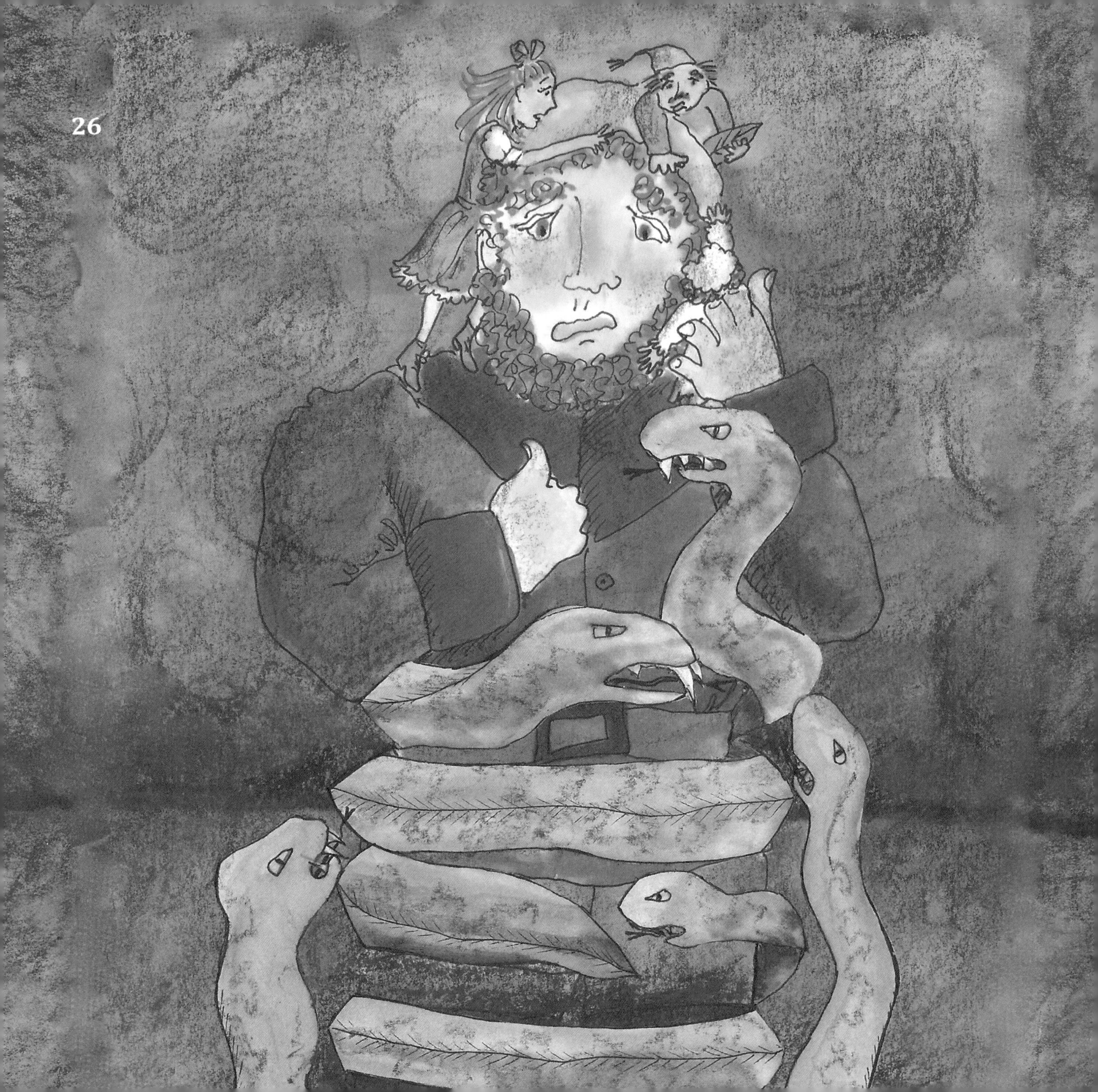

Then they heard the hiss of a spell. Before the giant could take another step, his feet were frozen to the ground by great snakes of ice slowly slithering up his legs and wrapping around his waist. The Light Princess and the dwarves began scrambling up his arms, heading to the top of his head. But on the way Mother Mizzle slipped, and in an instant was trapped in a cold coil on the giant's shoulder. Father Fizzle reached out his hand in vain, but dared not touch her lest the ice take him as well. The princess began to cry as her fingers and toes went numb. The giant began stuttering as the snakes circled around his chest. He cried out, "I m...m...miss my b...b...billy g...g...goat."

Then it happened. In spite of the dark and the danger, love for the giant welled up within the Light Princess, and she could not help herself: she giggled. Her fingers and toes were suddenly warm and Father Fizzle stared at her in wonder. "Your cheeks are rosy again. Laugh once more, child."

But the Light Princess was too scared, so Father Fizzle tried to help by telling her all the jokes he knew. She had heard all his jokes a thousand times before, so the princess could hardly manage a smile. However, the giant had never heard Father Fizzle's jokes, and he laughed his great, bumbling, sky-shaking laugh.

Soon the Light Princess began to giggle again. The more the giant laughed, the more the princess laughed, and finally Father Fizzle started laughing so hard that he could not keep telling jokes, but nobody needed to hear any more. They were laughing at themselves laughing. (You know how it is when you and your friends really get going with deep belly-laughs.)

They were all laughing so much that at first they did not notice the beams of light breaking through the mist, or their slithering bonds melting away. And in that magical laughing moment, as the blackness broke, the sun and the moon came out once more to dance and drive away the last strands of the mist. Even the smell of withering cabbage drifted away.

When the mist had disappeared and they looked down from atop the giant's head, they saw the wicked witch shaking her fist and shouting with the voice of only one angry rat. At that, they howled with laughter at the ridiculousness of the witch. The giant got so carried away that he lost his balance and stumbled, and they all heard a faint squish. The wicked witch was dead! The giant muttered, "Oh b...b...bother. Now I shall have to clean my b...b...boots." And they all laughed again.

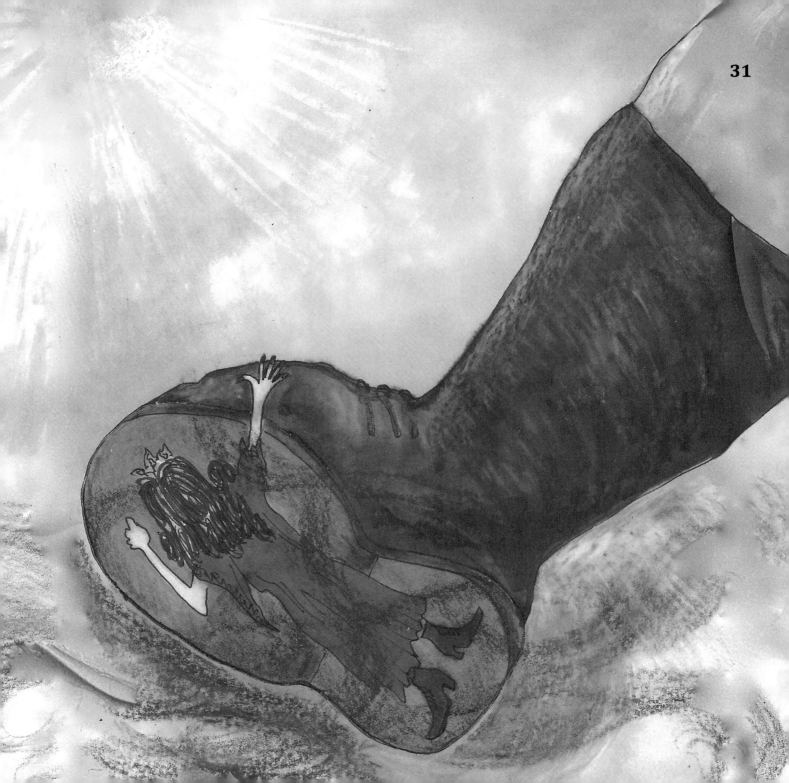

The kingdom was saved, and the giant sped toward the palace, carrying the Light Princess, Father Fizzle, and Mother Mizzle. Of course, this journey was infinitely better than the first one, and the princess cried and laughed as she heard stories of her parents and her kingdom from the dwarves. This time, the princess greeted all the creatures so cheerfully and kindly that they all followed the quartet. When the princess arrived in the capital city, she was at the head of the noisiest and least disciplined parade anyone had ever seen. But the queen, who was the first to recognize her daughter, declared it was the most honorable procession she had ever witnessed.

The reunion of the king and queen with the Light Princess and the dwarves was one of the happiest the kingdom had ever known. After several hours of talking, laughing, crying, hugging, and kissing, the princess furrowed her brow and asked why the whole kingdom was dressed so gloomily. The king and queen laughed, and the three of them scurried around, tearing down all the black banners and drapery and cutting up all their black clothing. The king ordered new horses be purchased and he and all his knights pulled out and polished their old armor from the royal treasury. The queen and her maidens found, hidden away deep in their wardrobes, colorful dresses for themselves and for the princess.

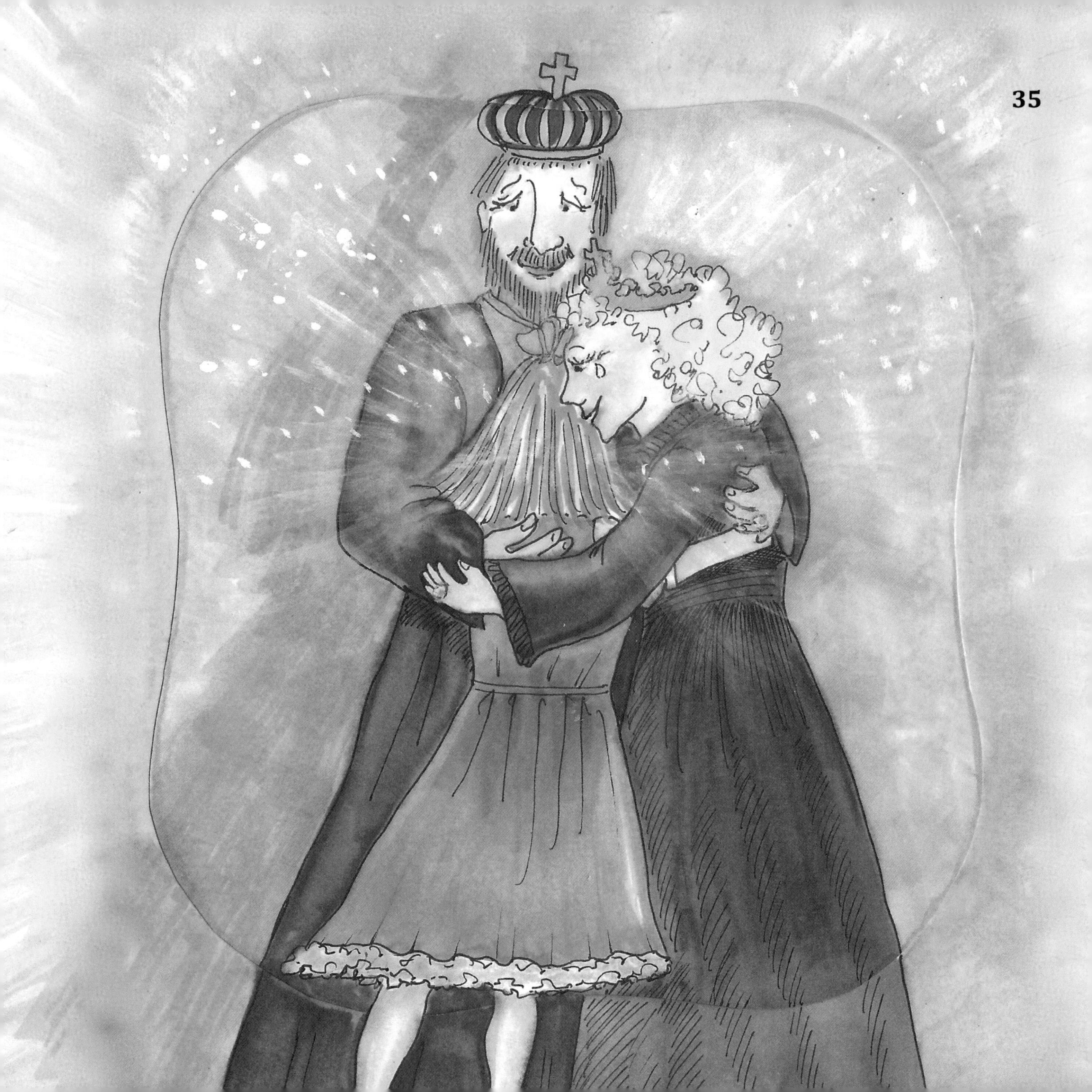

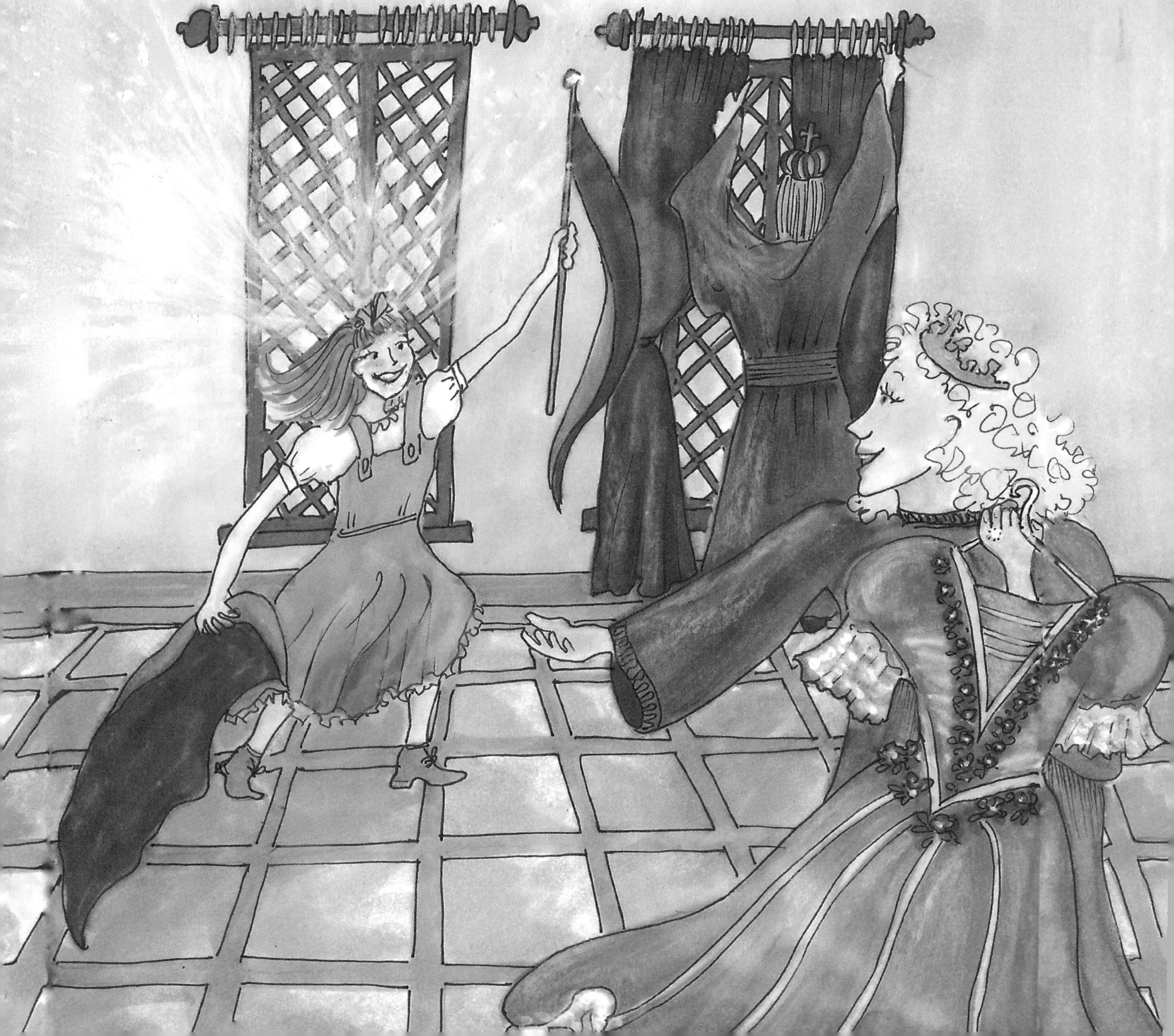

That night, the king and queen threw such a party, you would have thought another baby princess had been born. Fireworks lit the skies; the Pleiades led the dancing; the fauns had a tall task in keeping everyone's plates and glasses full of delightful foods and drinks. During the feast, the herald announced the return of the Light Princess in joyful, clear tones, and, with the king and queen, she went out among her people, and ate and drank and danced merrily.

There was no Maypole dance this time because Billy, the giant's billy goat, came bounding through and knocked the Maypole down, much to the dismay of the children. But the giant was so delighted to see his goat, and so funny in his delight, that the disappointed children soon started laughing. Riding Billy quickly became the highlight of the evening.

40 Among the fireworks and feasting and frolicking, the king and queen performed the very solemn ceremony of dubbing the giant First Knight of the Realm and Princess's Champion, and his newly-recovered billy goat was dubbed First Steed of the Realm. (Strictly speaking, this was bending the rules, because the First Knight is supposed to ride the First Steed, and the giant never rode Billy, much to Billy's relief, I'm sure. But, with all the children who rode on Billy's back that night, Billy probably was, overall, the most well-ridden and certainly the most well-loved steed in the realm.)

Father Fizzle and Mother Mizzle were named Chief Counselors of the Kingdom, and moved into the palace permanently, except for a month in the summer, when they returned to their rebuilt cottage in the woods. Often, the Light Princess went with them, and, oh, how she rejoiced in the sunrises and sunsets! Late into the nights, she charted the dances of the Pleiades.

And so the unhappy years spent in the shadow of the curse were ended. Never again did the people and buildings of the kingdom go about in black. Every year, they held a feast to celebrate the victory and return of the Light Princess, and everyone delighted in the wonderful fireworks, food, music, dancing, and billy goat riding! But nothing was as wonderful as when the Light Princess laughed. For all the fireworks and moonbeams and sunbeams in the world could not compare to the light that burst from her happiness.

About the Authors

Jordan and Leah Easley have been living and creating fairytales together for over ten years. They met in their first English literature class at Wheaton College and continued exploring stories at Gordon-Conwell Seminary. They currently live on an old chicken farm in coastal Maine, which, sadly, lacks a giant Billy goat named Billy. But they are ever on the lookout!

CPSIA information can be obtained
at www.ICGtesting.com
Printed in the USA
BVIC01n2034121213
338772BV00001B/2